<u>ICU</u>

I see you, head over hills ova a female
that is just a distraction.
She has you so snowed, you forgot all
your wants, hopes, and dreams
She places you in a hole deeper and
deeper.
She drains your emotions, yet the
intensive care you can place towards her
is hard to avoid.
Do you see him? He is trying to give you
all his energy.
You give him false hope of fantasy.
Do you see him and the units of energy
he sends to you almost daily?
You recognize the things he slows down
doing.
I see him, he requests the same of you,
but yet upon the request, you don't
oblige.
What do you want from him?
Nothing?!
You give him your availability for a
short period of time.
When it's convenient for you.

But, I see you leaving him even more
broken.
I see you
You are broken until you decide to let
your heartbreak.
It's intense to see you allow something
that has held so much weight to break.
You let the pieces fall, she fell amid the
break.
Don't pick her back up with the other
pieces.
She saw you in a shamble but only fed
her wants.
Everything else left, was trash to her.
Let her see you.
The one she broke to weakness but you
learned to build with strength.
The pieces are placed back and the holes
she left was filled with barriers of
solidity.
She saw you give more love than she
gave in return.
I see you become a piece of humbleness
and built a wall of protection.
I see you, breathing on your own.

<u>Roads</u>

Can we move forward?
Can it be fixed?
Moving forward while detours take
you on unusual paths.
The turns we take just to avoid the
collision.
How can the road be fixed, when we
steadily apply heavy pressure?
The cracks of emotions expand the
sinkhole.
Sunk in a position of lingering.
When you stuck, how can you move
forward?
Move forward by understanding that
the roads may shift.
Around the curves is the unknown.
Brace what's within when you release
pressure
Even on a bumpy road, the jerks will
fill the wakes of you.
You are still alive though.
The accident that occurred left you
with minor bruises.

The road you drove has been fixed.
The signs you tried to avoid are gone.
It's the same path.
You just need to drive it on cruise
control.
Learn your path.
You begin to see on the next journey.
The signs that you have there was
right.
The street was old and weary.
It is closed for renewal.
Next ride through, you will know how
to make it to your next destination.
You took your time and made it there
safely.

Undeniable

I am a vibe that can't be denied.
The aromatic smell of my strain will
keep you hypnotized.
The breeze from me will set you free.
Drift into the sounds of my lyrics.
Slide your fingers through the string
of my chords and loosen the tension.
Let's be honest that my clouds can
never be traced.
For in the shadows, the magnitude of
me shifts unexpectedly.
Never say you will catch me because
my stream can never reduce the speed
for the lack of your stability.
Even oil could never settle in a river
of the soulful carnal.
Even the drenched being of the falls
could not saturate the dryness of your
comfort.
The warmth of your cold nest cannot
heat a self-sufficient cave that I have
built on self-worth.

But yet and still you dug me enough
to find missing pipes laid away to
tarnish.
My lines refresh and aligned in
stealth.
What we flushed always recycles into
a strengthened amethyst crystal.
How did this charisma come back as
such a radiant stone?
I am the gem of the sea.
Worn by the goddess of
independence.
Not subtle to the opinions of the earth.
Unpredictable to the uncontrollable
moments I get in whimsical
encounters of storms.
The tornado of my fireworks is
tantalizing.
The glow of my purple reign is a
kaleidoscope attraction.
Once you hold it, look into my
tendencies.
Relinquish my aspiration is beyond
doubt.

<u>Wanna Feel</u>

I wanna feel your body next to me.

I wanna feel the heat of your body.

I wanna feel your chest rise as you inhale my pheromones.

I wanna feel your hand rubbing on my backbone and the ripple of my rib cage.

I have that extra piece you are missing from yours.

I wanna feel your lips, kiss me slowly in the crease of my neck.

I wanna feel your armor wrap itself around my wall.

I wanna feel the crumble of protection to the promise you will supply.

I wanna feel the strong thrust that makes the breath I breathe disappear.

I wanna feel like my overflowing ocean will never dry in a desert of despair.

I wanna feel the connection of our eyesight as I lock myself around the statue of your presence.

I wanna feel the lost memories return from the time the spot was found.

I wanna feel the sigh of relief as we raced to the finish line together.

I wanna feel the cool breeze as we intake a cold sensation.

I wanna feel the celebration as another turn hit a milestone.

I wanna feel the serenity of the essence as we did when we said hello.

Goodbye, I felt you.

Pearl

When she was picked, she was
handled with care.
The delicacy of her was rare amongst
the others in the garden.
The kind that comes in the era
specially made for a dark soul.
She was handed to him, promising to
submit to her scent that was built-in
growth.
Home is where they were alone, he
gazed at her as the time came.
He cleaned a place for her to lay,
fingers gliding through and through
the grains of her seeds.
As he touched, She began to crumble
by the heat of his fingertips.
Picking the petals of her, she lay
enduring the sensation.
Once you have done exploring the
beauty of the garden, he scooped her
up and began laying her in the bed.
Spreading every ounce of her being,
she felt the comfort of the browning
France scented sheets.

Holding her so tightly in, the stretch
of the sheets began to wrap,
swaddling for the beginning of
paradise she was soon to take him.
She is finally tucked in and ready for
the touch of his lips to take her in.
Her body is hot and ready to send the
explosion.
He looked at her deeply, admiring the
angles and how precise he wrapped
his present for this occasion.
He smiled at the peace of art he
created as he moved slowly in.
When his lips touched her tip, the
vibration sang "Take me in Baby".
He did, nice and slowly.
He released and looked at her.
She telepaths to his brain and asked,
"What's my name".
He said you are lustrous.
You are an unexplained expression.
You are PEARL.

<u>Status</u>

What is the status?

Is it positive that it is what is wanted?

Will it succumb to the negative of what
others will think?

What is the status?

Is it positive to the outcome it will behold
portraying despite life obstacles?

I have negative thoughts about what my life
would be like.

Something brought positivity and with the
presence of it, will everything work?

The positivity was never protected and the
infectious disease of infatuation spread
quickly.

The numbers were lost to negativity to
balance the debt of broken hearts.

Can you be positive to share your wants in
the field of the negative opposers?

Is it negative to think that the same sun that
shines so bright is the same moon that dims
on the sea of enchantment?

Being positive to protect the flesh but
negative to protect the heart.

Is the status positive it can withstand the
come upon of the negative of the told status?

What is the status accounted for?

The responsibility of being irresistible.

Statuses are left untold, shared in multiples
but hidden by few.

Tell the status and be positive that it is
negative.

Un-Wine

A day is a day to un-wine

Called in different directions

You whine for peace

The day is still moving

Time has come

Gasp for life as you breath

Volumizing the sound of thoughts

Settle down in the boudoir of serenity

Just get the time to un-wine

Grab the pearl stick that has been fumigated
by the scent of vanilla cream

Volume on ten percent, that didn't hit the
treble

Be bare to the openness of the breeze

Turn the volume to 11 percent, feel the beat
fade

Lay your burdens in the soapy accent of
lavender

Volume to 13 percent, feel the heartbeat to
the bass of your walls

Inhale the strawberry mint aromatherapy

Slide and look above the skylight

Escape to the planet of sacracy

Where you left the time to un-wine

Vibeology

There are certain criteria to match it

It is always unmatched

No matter how hard you try

It is a state of calmness

Its an era of chill

The energy is like no other

To be unbothered by irrelevance

There is no pretend

Relax in the midst of it

No details to unveil

It is the deed to go unorganized

Going with the flow at an all-time high

The aroma attracts the hungry

Feeding the significance that starves for
more

In the atmosphere of unacceptance

The presence is acceptable

It gives the steadiness to float and not come down

<u>Bridge</u>

He builds bridges you have to leap over to
get the obstacles he endures.

Is it impossible to cross his purpose without
closing the way?

Underneath him lies the storage of his truth.

He lets it be seen as he is the untruthful
artifact.

Never will he deny the probable clause
while searching for concealed changes.

He was built for strength to take any weight
that caused destruction.

Even small fragments from the environment
can cause his stance to shatter.

Holding on with all he used to be built
tearing him down with destruction that can't
be fixed.

Set up for failure his general purpose is
doomed from unfair retaliation.

Ruining his cause of life will not distinguish his capacity for growth.

The mindset he developed is hidden in the assumption of his tangled world.

He is a man that sets aside from wrongdoings and wants to carry over the envision of failed possibilities.

<u>Cute</u>

A woman is far more than cute.

She is attractive.

When she walks in your presence, her aura
attaches to whoever is close.

A woman is pretty.

When she steps, the endearing humor of her
stamina gives quality.

A woman is clever.

She quickly learns to understand that no one
computes her intelligence.

A woman is a self-seeking genius.

She sets high regard for her own happiness,
not easy to sacrifice her well being to please.

A woman seems to be superficial.

In reality just judged by those who share in
the worry of her next step, feeling left out.

A woman pleases all with the sight of her
statuesque.

She appeals to you with all the necessities.

A woman is indispensable.

She's an essential effect that can't be neglected.

So when you call her cute, realize the meaning.

Within it, she is all the building components for such a simple word.

Molded

Raised bold to never depend on man was
what a young Queen did.

Don't be warmed by their touch, be cold as
their heart.

Work for the wants of desire.

Fall to their knees to know your needs.

Walk upright for admiration.

Lay downward in respect and approval.

Raised to be a queen, find the king for your
mold.

A King is searching for his Queen in raising.

When he finds her, the two will sacrifice
their mold at the alter of their royal
ancestors.

The King mold sided by the Queen mold.

He will lay in her mold as she will lay in his.

Royal ancestors will begin to pray.

The prayer for life, health, strength, truth,
wellness, and prosperity.

The heirs of the new kingdom will begin to grow and fulfill the mold.

They shall rise together.

He takes her hand and will stand amongst the royals.

The prayers have been set.

They have been molded to stand and fight for their people.

King, lead his Queen.

Clear her path of disturbance and interference.

Stand beside her for if she leans, his arms will grab hold and stand her up.

Never fall behind unless to admire the creation of the mold.

She should never look back at what has failed her.

Queen, as he leads and clears the path walk firmly on the gold walkway of her destiny.

When it feels heavy and the tower leans, she will go in the direction of the King and his armor protection.

She will never look back when she has been failed.

The kingdom depends on their strength.

When the affirmation prayer has been set.

King and Queen are blessed by the throne.

They sit high to never look low.

They will run a bonded kingdom by strength.

Their determination, mindset, and abilities are molded to not be broken.

The royals will offer their introduction.

For many has come before and didn't fit the mold and some were forced in only for the thought of the title but not to uphold the role.

Royal ancestors specially built this kingdom mold and kept it locked.

To unlock the mold, the hearts of the raised youngs had to beat on one accord.

Hearts are broken free from hindrance.

They are raised to find each other, the time it took to strengthen for the mold.

Stand and observe the structure created and the boldness of the mold they will uphold.

Molded together.

Rain Chatter

Ever in the element of rain.

Listen clearly as the drops make a sound.

Give them your thoughts and listen.

The response is transparent.

Listen to the clicks it gives in your ears.

A calming alarm you are yet to hear.

They ask why such despair in the air you
breathe.

Peace will sign the agreement of your needs.

The midst comes to cradle your defense.

Inhale the stream and drown the doubt.

Release the bough and break it into pieces.

Wetness soaks through the bandages and
deteriorates the stitches.

Smell the sweetness of the natural well.

Given hydration to purify the zone.

Think no more of the uncertainty.

A clear view of certain wash for a
transparent sight.

Your Eyes

It is something about your eyes.

It tells a story of desire.

You release your vision to me.

Hold me in your arms and take it in.

You missed me for some time, I overthink your feelings.

Sometimes they are stronger than before.

My insecurities make me feel like you have had enough.

Have I done all that you have required of me?

Am I doing the job right?

Looking in your eyes.

The ones I use to can read.

Sometimes it's not as legible.

Daily you keep it so thorough with me.

You keep the same routine with us.

Your eyes on my foundation, you admire so
much.

I still ask, What is it about me?

Why do you still want me?

When you take a swim, you dive into the
deepest that the pool allows.

I lay enjoying the sound of your
uncertainties.

It's the sound that shows the wondering of
the next moves.

It is then in your eyes, I realize we are in
that moment.

Being Dark

Born in the realm of a confused gloom.

Separated by the tone of your absence.

Is it because the dark can be unseen?

Realize after dark brings to light.

Darkness gives illumination for brightness.

With low tones, the set of highlights
presents a glow.

Focus on the shade, when you concentrate
you can locate the beauty within.

The names that have bestowed on the
characteristic poorly disguises the
manifestation.

Through dark brings relaxation, finding the
absence hidden within.

Close eyes to dark to see the admiration of
your glow dancing in self-conscious glory.

Be compassionate to the wall that darkness
provides, protectant of the encounters that
are terrified to be seen.

Beyond the beauty of tenebrous obscurity,
even the overcast of clouds will separate it
from fraying.

Overthink

The only thing we need to control is our overthinking.

If we going to overthink anything, let us overthink our self-esteem.

Hype up your own worth, even when you have to do it alone.

Things happen when you want them to happen.

Think of you first, you live for you first.

Self-love only works when you learn to love yourself.

Everything isn't what it seems, but because of your mind, you allow it to think over.

If it doesn't happen as it should, realize it's ok.

Be ok with having no control.

Randomness to life can be a necessity.

Getting used to the same routine should get lame sometimes.

If you overthink anything, overthink insecurities with positivity.

Be positive to know that everything works out accordingly.

A reaction to the unknown for sure will cause a reaction to a certain answer you built within.

Release that pressure of boundness.

Take an ease and clear the negativity.

Everyone doesn't move accordingly every time.

It is not what you think.

It is only because you think.

When there is no actual cause, never let it affect the effection.